Oh Me Oh I Oh You...just ask the questions

Second Edition

Grace Asphall

Oh Me Oh I Oh You...just ask the questions

Introduction

The idea of writing this book was founded on the people whom I have met on the streets or in an establishment in my Flatbush neighborhood in Brooklyn, New York, USA. I summed them up as being bold and strapped with interesting character traits. They never cease to amaze and impress me with their antics, stories, knowledge on world events, laws, local happenings and their opinions on current affairs and religion. They court stamina. More importantly they express themselves without fear...self-induced therapy.

Oh Me Oh I Oh You...just ask the questions

Acknowledgement

I am grateful to a few of my past colleagues who were constantly amused by my spin on any news report, article or literature. Sometimes they even labeled me *funny lady*, which I don't see myself as one. But if at the end of the day I can make someone smile it would have worth my living. Besides calling me *funny lady*, they pestered me to do a blog and of course I always ignored them. I told them no because my information would be lost among the who's who clan. My response meant nothing to them. All they were interested in was to see me start a blog. Ultimately, I delivered a blog: www.fromheretotherewithgrace.com I do not live there as often as I should or used to be because I am busy in my new role as a retiree; and belief me retirement is no *Golden Years* as touted. It is a pain in the behind literally and physically, having to chase proper healthcare and insurance.

I am also grateful to some of my Facebook audience, family and friends who have encouraged me in my inherent behavior: sweet antics. People sometimes become complacent, fall asleep at the wheel so to speak. Therefore, my faint nudge be it in the form of a question or an opinion is guaranteed to keep everyone alert. An educator once told me that a journalist, communications expert and a talk show host should always put themselves in the place of the audience. Think like them for a moment and ask the questions that you think they would ask.

My Facebook family, you are copacetic. I listened to those who placed their requests for a book and would be a spoilsport not to deliver. So here's to all the requests! In the same spirit: to those who cannot control their laughter and giggles while reading my posts on the subway; to those who sneak and read them elsewhere and find themselves in the same situation; to the ladies who read the posts at home and frighten their husbands with raucous laughter, leading them to suspect me for such behavior everytime; please continue to update me. LOL! LMAO! And I hope that Facebook lives on.

Laughter is the best medicine.

Oh Me Oh I Oh You…Just ask the questions

Second Edition

Grace Asphall

Flatbush

Flatbush! Perhaps bushy and rural would be the initial thoughts for those who have not visited this community in Brooklyn, New York, USA. Even if this has a ring of truth to it, rest assured that it has been said that good things come from the bush. Much respect Flatbush! To what you were before by nature, in between and what you are today.

In my spare time, during employment, I had a habit of viewing and enjoying the scenes and activities in my Flatbush neighborhood. Now that I have been blessed with retirement from a job of over 30 years, I decided to spend the greater portion of my time profusely combing the neighborhood and talking with strangers, some of whom I now consider friends. I have met the homeless. I have met the talkative. I have met the lonely. I have met the ferocious. I have met those who claimed that they had had it all: the American dream by their standards and lost it all, left with nothing. I have also met the chic, churl, shy, tricky, lame, professional, auxiliary, haughty, beggars, needy, pretenders, complainers, warmongers, the religious, the political, the bargain hunters, higglers, vendors, storekeepers, the coupon goddesses, the fortune tellers, the food pantry goers and comics. Although some of the people I have met are like fleeting dreams, never to be seen again, believe it or not, every Jackman that I have interacted with has left an impression in my mind. Their stories, conversations, mannerisms, farsightedness, depth, and operations have become major lessons to me. A floor plan. A wealth of knowledge. And a guarded belief that no one is too old to learn.

My Flatbush community is a kisser, kickass, badass, sucker and a delight; always been. I have been romancing it for over thirty years through thick and thin. People who endured Flatbush back in the nineteen eighties are said to be tough. Well, I am not tough. There were days when I came close to pissing my drawers, by brute force. Like the time in the early nineteen eighties when I was held in an elevator at knife point and robbed. The sun on that day beamed in all its glory. Radiant! Yet it became dim in my mind as my assailant fondled me, and I thought he would triturate my vagina. It was horrible! His dirty hands! His handsome evil looks. His fair skin flushed with bad blood. I wanted to live. He flipped my breasts from my brassiere as if they were flip charts. The brazen thief stole an Enicar Watch that my mother had given me. He also stole my couple dollars and token and had the nerve to tell me to walk with more money next time. He pointed the knife at me as he backed out of the elevator and told me not to scream until he made his getaway. But the minute he left, the elevator took me to another floor where a tenant jumped in and saw my disheveled and frightened appearance. He asked what happened. I told him someone robbed me, and he jumped back out of the elevator and ran down the stairs, but by then the thief was only a wind. Police and neighbors rushed to the scene when a further alarm was made. It was a scary moment in that nineteen eighties time. At this point, I pause to express gratitude to my friends Audrey Wright and Dr. Doret Wright-Ledford who rushed home as fast as they could to console me.

Robbery had become a fad. How else can it be described? The other time was in the early nineteen nineties when I arrived home from work just in time to see a burglar leaving my apartment. He even had the nerve to greet me with *good afternoon*, and asked me the time as he held his stuffed coat pockets with authority. I answered him politely, pretending as if I didn't see him closing the door to my apartment. I was fearful so I played along. On entering the apartment I realized that the crook had gone through every crevice and corner. Drawers, clothes and papers were on the floor. I felt violated. The television was unplugged and looked ready to be transported. He stole my gold-plated necklace and its fish pendant I had just received for my birthday. I was furious! I was even more furious when I noticed he had folded one of my birthday cards to hold the door in place as he left. And of course I had to spend extra money to change my door lock.

I also recall the days when the sounds of shots firing from guns had everyone frozen in place, trying to figure out its direction instead of running to seek shelter. My friends and family were concerned about me living in what was like the wild west. People had no regards for life. They did what they wanted to do. I recall the September, Monday, a Labor Day holiday, again in the early nineteen nineties. My two daughters had spent the night at one of my neighbor's, on another floor of our dwelling. They had left just in time that day to return to my apartment and to escape a bullet from a drive-by shooting, which nestled in the bed where they had slept the night before. The guns blazed often especially on the weekend. Sirens wailed and helicopters rumbled and hovered above buildings. We anticipated the discharge of a gun on a Sunday afternoon as if it were a grand sports or cookies and ice cream treat. Whenever my younger daughter heard the gunshots, she would say *get flat mommy*, aiming for under the dining table.

Still, I remained in my Flatbush neighborhood and weathered the storms of discontent, chaos and bad blood. My children survived. I survived. Some neighborhood dwellers were not so fortunate. Occasionally, a few pop-pops broke the silence. And one wondered if the pop-pops were really gunshots, or just firecrackers. Beyond that, I am happy that I stayed in my Flatbush neighborhood to see the massive and important changes. It has become a highly diverse neighborhood. The social gravity and enjoyment are even greater now. Today, the chance of hearing a barrage of gas bubbles leaving the body is much greater than the sound of shots being fired from a gun. Flatbush is a sought-after neighborhood where you need lots of money to rent an apartment or purchase a property. The location is great. Public transportation is great, and you can find cuisines from different nations well represented. Flatbush is alive!

Saying: Clear conshens sleep wen it a tunda.
Translation: Clear conscience sleeps while
there is thunder.
Meaning: People with clear consciences can
sleep through the stormiest nights.

Radiant day - Flatbush, Brooklyn, NY.

Old sayings and culture now stand up to a new culture.

Every culture under the sun embraces aphorisms. From the Caribbean to Africa to Europe to Asia to North America, name any country, city and region of the world and there are bound to be sayings. In Jamaican culture there is always an adage to fit or describe any situation or concern. To the people who fear that all is lost, just think about the old adage: *there is a plaster to fit every wound*. Somehow, somewhere whatever the case is, there is an answer. There is a plan. There is a solution. Or, sometimes a groan. Groans speak volumes so don't treat them with a bad attitude.

I remember giggling at the sayings when they were dispensed by my parents as a warning or reprimand. I remain grateful that my laughter didn't paint me as being insolent, which could have been easily calculated as that. Because when parents speak in their role children should listen; at least that was the order of the day back then. Above all though, I wanted to know what the sayings meant. But my parents held the translations hostage and made it known:

pig did ask him mummah why har mouth suh long. And

di mummah seh tuh him, by and by yuh a grow come yuh wi si.

That was one of the funniest things I had ever heard and even to this day I always smile whenever I see a long-mouth pig. In essence, my parents and the elders in the village were trying to say that as age increases, experience is the master teacher.

The elders who used sayings didn't warrant the labels: miserable and crazy old people. In hindsight they were philosophers in their own rights. Because as life experiences unfolded the meanings of the adages were exposed. The repertoire of sayings was a part of the plan in my grooming. To take care of me in later years. Those adages have become my lifeline. A good dose of medicine for the mind, especially as technology manipulates man and man manipulates technology.

Also, without the shadow of a doubt, the eccumenical prints of modern times are scary. It must be the boogeyman that is out to get unruly children. As a matter of fact the boogeyman is getting everyone these days in the form of lucified technology. Sometimes it's hard to digest or even acknowledge the changes and upgrades which are great yet can be to our detriment if not handled properly. Already social media and texting has eroded physical interaction; people hardly speak to each other any more. There is an air of moral decay. It's frightening that a child will be with a parent yet will have a conversation via texting instead of speaking to the parent. How on earth did family time morph into a silent world? Can you imagine if our foreparents should be tested with this method? I think they would faint and die again because in their minds and hearts to have a child texting and not speaking to an adult, no matter who they are, would be intolerant.

Look around and you will notice that there is an acute anomie taking place. The way we usually greet each other has been tampered with. Nobody seems to pay much attention to the absence of *good morning, good day, good afternoon, good evening and good night.* The world is moving fast, changes are rapid and curt moves seem to be more acceptable. No lingering; just say what you have to say and keep things moving. The behavior has opened grounds for the quickest way to greet each other. Hence to say *hello*, *hey* and *hi* doesn't stir anger like they did in the past. Neither are they viewed as impolite or rude.

At the end of the day it doesn't matter the words used to convey a greeting because it guarantees a personable expression will follow in the form of a question. Two popular ones are: a) *How are you doing*? b) *How are you*? Responding to a simple question after a greeting can start many conversations. Having said that, the highpoint to this book is asking questions. In my juvenile years a popular response to a question was: *Ask me no questions and I will tell you no lies*. It sounded comical but at the same time could be measured as a scare tactic to the people who were in the habit of asking questions. Can you imagine what the world would be like if there were no questions?

Many moons ago, while in an office procedures class, the instructor imparted that a good secretary never relies on memory. Everything is written down somewhere. The challenge from this day forward is to jot down questions as they surface. Time will grant space for them to be asked.

Saying: The proof of the pudding is in the eating.
Meaning: Test something to get the true experience.

Is there magic in asking questions?

I recall sitting at a public facility when out of the blue a lady looked at me and asked, "Have you ever kept two men at the same time?"
"No", I quickly answered, feeling shocked.
"Me too", she said, looking into space.

In the meantime my mind raced in all directions, thinking like a virago about her boldness in seeking intimate details about me. Did she see the words *variety of men* or roast duck, lizard lap and missionary positions stamped on my forehead? Did she see condoms dangling from my earlobes? Or, was she of the opinion that my pumpum (vagina) was placed in the palm of my hand? I would expect that juggling two men in an intimate fashion would subject my pumpum to much pressure, wear and tear and stress. Adding to that a statutory kiss from everyone could prove unhealthy. Saliva isn't wine or lemonade. Like me, this lady, Sally will be her name, was a familiar face at the facility. She exhibited a raucous persona which didn't scare me. And interestingly, we had had numerous conversations before but not about my love life. Furthermore, I am tough underneath my easy going appearance. I keep my cards close to my chest when it comes to my intimate relationship. I do not kiss and tell.

It took Sally a few seconds to speak again after placing a ditto on my response to her question. Dating more than one man at the same time was also a profound no for her. In the same breath she also expressed a feeling of unfaithfulness. I narrowed my eyes at her. *She must be a troubled woman*, I thought. Frightened by the look on my face she quickly explained that her unfaithfulness is associated with working for two separate agencies. A careless laugh escaped me. Vulgar! For all the tea in China I wouldn't have guessed that the question, she posed to me, about dating more than one man at the same time was based on the way she earns her income.

Saying: Alligator lay egg but him nuh fowl.
Translation: Alligator lays egg but it is not a fowl.
Meaning: Things are not always as they seem.

Did Sally use me as a guinea pig when she asked me if I had ever dated two men at the same time? Sally reminded me of a mischievous child. I felt like slapping her on her hand for picking my brain to get to her purpose. I figured through conversations she is a street-smart person but didn't think about that when she threw the question at me.

Anyway, I keenly listened to her as she continued talking about her *strange unfaithfulness*. She stated that on her arrival to America she worked with an agency which gave her a good start in life but didn't have much benefits. No 401K or union benefits. So she sneaked off to sign up with another agency which allowed her the benefits she craved for. The agencies in her eyes were like having two men, two lovers. I was astonished at the comparisons drawn by Sally. To add to that she mentioned that a few days after she had signed up with agency number two, faith had it that agency number one, *her first love*, suited her with an assignment which she declined without an explanation. Her intention though is to still remain with agency number one. According to her she could never find it in her heart to leave it. I then said to myself, if I am involved in any indiscretion, this is the kind that would interest me. Sign up with multiple agencies so that I could fend for myself and not depend on others who may want me to repay them in coin or kind.

Saying: Nuh listen tuh di nize. Watch di sale.
Translation: Don't listen to the noise. Watch the sale.
Meaning: Do not be duped by the excitement. Investigate the facts to judge something for yourself.

Is Sally a deep thinker, a religious or honest person to have asked me about dating two men at the same time? When Sally posed her question to me about dating two men at the same time, the thought crossed my mind: she was a little strange. But in that moment as I listened to her talking about her situation, working with two agencies, I could see that she was struggling with her conscience. I damned myself in my mind for not being a psychologist, counselor or whatever the label is. This would allow me to officially triage, diagnose and prescribe. Possibly put Sally in a straight jacket or give her a piece of paper and a pencil and tell her to draw her family, the church she attends and a frightening experience. Not being qualified, I figured the use of adages would be an alternative to handle her concern. Back in the day, the elders used adages to coach, prepare, console and reassure people when necessary. Sally deserved to hear the importance of bending her mind to her condition. *People with raw meat should seek fire for themselves.* And that *she should not carry all her eggs in one basket* because should that basket fall it's likely that all the eggs would be broken. It would leave her with none.

Saying: Do not judge a book by its cover. Meaning: Study a person's behavior before making any assertions.

Are sayings sufficient to show Sally the difference between working with two agencies and dating two men at the same time? Listen up Sally! Some women will keep two intimate boyfriends and reap benefits whereas some in the same position will receive zilch. Nothing! So that Sally further understands what's going on on a broader spectrum, I seized the moment to rant and share with her a little piece of American experience since she wasn't fully seasoned to the way things can be. She was still a newcomer in my sight. It's possible that she will encounter nothing alarming or unfortunate. Nonetheless, it's still imperative to let her know that in America people seldom give away anything, especially money. It's not a bed of rose in America as most people think. And God forbid if Sally leans towards becoming a public charge. The government agencies, regardless of whether they decide on giving any help, all of a sudden would want to act as if they are internists, based on the personal questions they may ask. They must know about all the children, husband, family. And it is expected too that a widow's mite have to be declared or even a fowl coop if there is ownership on one. Government agencies want to know everything and in the process will leave no stone unturned even if it takes a decade to get the information. They are diggers. They will gather details about your mama and your mama's mama. Gather details from your neighbors, friends and Parson too if necessary. *The whole kit and kaboodle.* Therefore, working with two agencies to suit needs is acceptable. It's the best way to financial stability and freedom.

Saying: Puss an dwag nuh have di same luck.

Translation: Puss and dog do not have the same luck.
Meaning: People with similar situations experience different outcome.

Have I benefited from Sally's question about dating two men at the same time? The interaction between Sally and I was refreshing. I am glad I exhibited no bad attitude towards her. Neither did I shun her question which turned out to be a teachable moment for me. Some people with little or no credentials at all are extremely sharp in their thinking. Don't underestimate their judgement, potentials and common sense. Sitting down in silence with questions swirling around in your head does not bring relief until they are asked. Sally didn't even test the waters with me, exploring my temperament, before she shot her question at me. Instead, she was rather direct. According to Granny, *mongoose seh if yuh nuh tek chance yuh a nuh man.* It's possible that Sally had fancied this Jamaican saying which by now should have reached the north pole or somewhere in Antarctica. Jamaicans are not afraid to take their culture with them wherever they go. They are as daring as a mongoose.

Saying: Book learning a nuh intelligence.
Translation: Book learning is not intelligence.
Meaning: An educated person can be lacking
in common sense.

Is the mongoose a strange creature?

It is rather noteworthy to say that as a child I learnt that the mongoose was imported to Jamaica to rid the island of its dangerous snakes. Over the years the story went on to say that the mongoose protected the cane fields from rats. I will not dispute or argue about its purpose in Jamaica because one thing I know for sure, the mongoose will enter the yard of a dwelling during daylight and snatch a chicken in full view of people.I have seen that daring action by the mongoose many times during my childhood and had often wondered why this creature acts so boldly. The mongoose will also run across the street without looking up or down for any oncoming traffic, sometimes getting killed. A stark reminder of the misfortunes that can engulf us when we are not alert and aware of our surroundings. Or, even during an attempt at our personal goals.

Saying: Luk before yuh leap.
Translation: Look before you leap.
Meaning: Make sure that there will be no
repercussion from your action.

Should the mongoose be embraced?

During childhood, inasmuch as the mongoose protected us from harmful snakes, I still viewed it as a scoundrel, a crook, a flipping thief because it steals chickens. But let's not focus on the bad habit of this creature. Let's sincerely look at the trait which encourages people to aim for what they want.

Saying: In the best of us there is a little bad and in the worst of us there is a little good.

Would I take daring chances like the mongoose?

I would take chances if push comes to shove but hope it would not be for the worse. Also, it's not a bad thing to get out of my comfort zone to experience something different. The adage *A rolling stone gathers no moss* is in sync with modern times. It's useless to stagnate with all the increase in technology. Always be on the move, seeking new locations. And in doing so, inadvertently force stumbling blocks out of the way. How about you, would you take chances of any sort?

Saying: Nothing beats a trial but a failure.

Should your questions be infused with diplomacy?

Hello! We all have pet peeves! Please don't test my asperity with the word diplomacy. I always view it as a temporary treatment to situations. Ulterior motive. It's like medication. It treats symptoms but does nothing to fix the illness. Cut that diplomacy crap which in bygone days was referred to as sweet talk, a tongue of deceit. Be direct with me. Tell me the truth. No made-up conniving, selfish stuff. No Bamboozling. Why would anyone opt to remain fooled or tricked for a period of time? Isn't working out a peaceful solution much better than entering an agreement that could easily backfire?

Looking at diplomacy on a broader spectrum, it is understandable that some people are sensitive, very hard to deal with and have a fragile ego. Hence, caution should be exercised when dealing with them. And there are also those who would rather remain in denial than hear the truth or even an opinion. Some people will read this view about diplomacy and call it folderol. That's reasonable given the fact that everyone shares different views

One day while holding a conversation with a relative

about diplomacy, he referred to a quote by Will Rogers, an American entertainer: *Diplomacy is the art of saying nice doggie until you can find a rock*. I laughed hard when I heard him relayed it. At the rate diplomacy is being used, if we take Will Rogers' statement seriously, there will be very little rocks left on the land.

Saying: Nuh hide yuh tick an lick man.
Translation: Do not hide your stick and hit man.
Meaning: Be honest from the beginning when dealing with someone.

Should some people be blatantly barred from asking questions because of their social standing?

The workers at oval, round, oblong, rectangle or square offices who sit importantly in swivel chairs and roll around from one end of the desk to the next, are deemed astute. It's also easy to tell when they are at the pinnacle in a company. You will see them sit with their chairs reclined, feet on desks and pretending to bite the tops of their pens to give the impression that they are really thinking about solutions. Behind their backs they are called *biggies, big-shots* or *top guns*. They are held in high regards and their work viewed as brilliant. They are there as decision-makers and to ask questions. But sometimes they are swept away by portfolios and labels that they will ask questions and answer them without giving others the opportunity to do so. In moments like those a remote control for humans would be a welcome threat.

Bosses or *biggies,* most used label, are so used to having the upper hand in situations that it's impossible for them to think otherwise. Maybe they see themselves as creators of great questions and the only ones who can ask them. It's easy to equate them with the saying: *when I speak no dogs bark. Biggies* paint a picture in their audiences' minds, a perceptive approach to their asking questions. Sometimes they will transport you on an imaginary round trip to Hawaii or some other place, so to speak, before getting to the heart of a situation or a question they have in mind. In the end they are disappointed because their audience delivers spurious answers due to overthinking.

Biggies even play psychologists before they ask questions. They use a term called *icebreakers* otherwise known as fun things to *warm up* their audience. If I should look at the situation from a scientific or environmental angle, it is unnecessary to chase *glaciers* with *icebreakers* in an age of global warming. Likewise, people will participate during the course of a gathering depending on the delivery by the moderator or speaker. People will react to their own personal climate, anyway. Going to work is not going to a social club. There is a reason for *Happy Hour* after work. People shouldn't be at work learning to play games. They are not in kindergarten. Sometimes psychology, if used by the wrong person, can be a bitch especially if it is the cheap kind.

Back in the day the person at the helm of a meeting didn't require leadership training because common sense and good grooming prevailed. They would bring store bought cookies, bun and cheese or bulla/cake and then announced that the undivided attention of everyone is necessary. Food makes everyone happy. It is the staff of life. Also, it is said: *you catch more flies with honey than you do with vinegar.*

Compare the *biggies* to a subordinate who asks questions. It's most likely the subordinate will be told that the question is irrelevant or to postpone questions until another time. An ordinary person must have stamina to ask questions or face dismissal prematurely or even laughed at. If push should come to shove, the ordinary person can bring new light and growth in a difficult situation. They often think outside of the box. They engage in critical thinking whereas astute people deal mostly with booksense.

It's understandable that most times people are tactless in asking questions or collecting information. But believe me the ordinary people without portfolio or title have an ineffable way of diffusing nerves with their tactile approach. It is said that *God protects fools and babies*. Never doubt ordinary people in their approach on how to seek information, deliver information, put questions in the proper context and more importantly, how to deliver gossip. They do not need to consult Google, neither take you on an imaginary trip. Neither would they consult their mamas and papas. Instead, they use the common sense they are blessed with to conduct business. For example, let's say John and Mary are best friends, bosom buddies. And John heard something that would besmirch Mary's character. In his approach he would say, *Mary I am going to tell you something but I do not want you to get mad. You are my friend and if I hear anything bad about you I am going to tell you.* An approach such as this will encourage Mary to listen.

The methods of the ordinary people are just as debonair as the *biggies, top guns, big shots* or any other names you may choose to use. According to the elders, *One monkey cannot run the show.* Teamwork, diversity and unity is imperative. *A plane cannot fly on one wing. In the same manner one hand cannot kill lice.*

Saying: What's good for the goose;
is also good for the gander.
Meaning: Everyone should be treated equally.

Are you guilty of holding in questions in the same manner as your farts?

Back in the day children were told not to hold their wind because it had caused the death of Mary

Lee. The tombstone of Mary Lee is located on the main road in Lacovia, St. Elizabeth, Jamaica. Rumor has it that Mary Lee refused to break wind because of her pride. For good manners she could have released her wind in a discreet manner. Clear her throat, moved a chair noisily, coughed or lay blame on a nearby dog. Or, if it came on a rush, without warning, she had the opportunity to say excuse me and play deaf to the giggles around her. Instead she still held her pride and the belief that passing wind was a nasty and disrespectful thing to do. As a result, it cost her her life. Years later, going into my adulthood, the tombstone story changed from the remains of Mary Lee to a man and his horse. The new information changed nothing because by then Mary Lee's story had become a warning: *Let fart be free because it is the death of poor Mary Lee.*

Not allowing your bodily functions to take a natural course could be detrimental to your health. There is a reason for an exhaust pipe on a vehicle. It's essential in carrying away waste gas from the engine for good mileage. Likewise, relieve yourselves of questions. Don't be afraid to ask questions even if someone looks at you cross-eyed or with disgust. Or, even label you nosey.

Ask and it shall be given. Seek and you shall find, according to the scriptures. The mind is inquisitive. *An idle mind is the devil's workshop* so put it to good use. Also remember that the *world wide web* (www) has the strangest ability to expose our every nook and cranny whether or not we like it. Therefore, now is not the time to be shy about anything especially when there is a crisis.

Ask questions! If you see someone with a book that you would love to have, please don't take it without asking if you can have it. You will be labeled a thief when you take people's belongings without their permission. Never take for granted that you are entitled to people's items or you can do as you please just because you are friends with the owner. Questions show respect. Good manners. Questions open minds. And it is in knowing that one shall understand. Questions can remove roadblocks. Questions are not limited to one set of people, or to a certain class or hue. They are for everyone to appease their minds.

Keep in mind too that people's understanding and level of education vary. There is an expression which states: *to assume is to make an ass of you and me*. The elders from back in the day would have said, *seven brothers; seven different minds.* Everyone is not from the same fabric or social standing. However, it's equally important to know our written thoughts can be edited or translated without losing flavor and purpose. Do not sit and let anyone brainwash you into believing that stupid questions exist. No such thing! Questions have rights, ask them with gusto and pride. Even if you are plagued with bad grammar, spoonerism and malapropism. Ask them. Some people may giggle but look at it as putting a smile on their faces.

Adding to that, society often dictates several ways to ask questions. But while keeping that in mind as a show of formality, do not be bullied into saying or doing something that doesn't express your true feelings or address your concerns. Say it the best way you can. Someone will understand. And according to Granny, *it's not what you ask but how you ask it.* Speak with respect. But also, as a rule of caution, *when the lion is sleeping don't try to wake him.* Inasmuch as you are eager to unload your concerns; know and learn to identify when people are not feeling up to par to get involved.

Saying: Empty pots cannot boil over.

Meaning: Do not let your concerns fester until they become outbursts.

Are you always uncomfortable in the presence of a learned person?

Chances are you will understand the language of an educated person if you are equally educated. Those who are not in the league of the erudite will find that sometimes it's best to sit and listen during a conversation. If you must do otherwise choose to smile and nod importantly. Try not to embarrass yourselves by participating in a conversation if you are hearing a word for the first time. I was at a bar in my early twenties, when a story was told about a man with limited vocabulary. He arrived home to see his wife in their matrimonial bed in an uncompromising position with a strange man. In a shocked state he angrily asked the perpetrator what he was doing on top of his wife. The perpetrator eased himself on one elbow and in a scholarly tone he expressed to the husband that he was having sexual intercourse with her. The answer came as a relief to the husband. He threw his hands up in praise and said to the clever perpetrator, "thank God because I thought you were fucking her".

On the other hand, an educated person sometimes speaks with a high-falutin tongue, not so much as to impart knowledge but to hear how they sound, show off, boycott the ordinary person's voice or trick them with big words. Big words always seem to be the key card among such people. Or, at least that's what they believe. It should be observed that a person who is not the brightest star in the galaxy can count on intuition or gut feeling and their impeccable common sense. For example, a large-scale farmer in a certain village in Jamaica who was illiterate found himself in the presence of a few educated men who were holding a conversation. They were using big words and having a grand time, confident that the farmer wouldn't understand. But it didn't take long for truth to hit them when the farmer revealed to the erudite men he knew they were talking about him. He told them that although he couldn't read and write, he had the ability to "smell words", understand their meanings.

Saying: Man nuh dead; nuh call him duppy.

Translation: Man that isn't dead; do not call him duppy.
Meaning: Don't underestimate people's potential.

Do you find questions that should benefit you upsetting, or is it the person asking the questions?

The questions you ask today could produce positive change tomorrow or even save lives. They induce comfort, expose truths and bring about many *Aha* moments. By the same token, asking too many questions can annoy people without patience or tolerance. For example, have you ever been to the Doctor with an unbearable pain and the doctor keeps asking you the same questions over and over? In that moment you are disgusted and find you are on the verge of becoming blasphemous; at will to use the famous profanities: fuck and rass as determined by society. (The topic profanity is for another time especially when it is a given or family name).

Most times a medical condition requires immediate care and is not a time to entertain questions. But it's good to note that there is always a method to a doctor's madness. Malpractice lawsuits are a doctor's nightmare. Equally important is to see a patient restored to good health. Treat yourself well so that others can do the same. Without self-respect it is easy to become disrespectful. Self-respect begets patience too and is an important ingredient for balance. It has been said numerous times that *patience is a virtue*. Or, *patient man rides the donkey*, according to the old adage. Never be always in a hurry. Do things in the right manner to get good results.

Saying: Sick nuh care; dacta worse.
Translation: Sick doesn't care; doctor doesn't care either.
Meaning: If you don't care about your problems don't expect others to care.

Is recess noted on your daily schedule?

When I was a child, I looked forward to recess time at school. Continuous classroom work without breaks is unhealthy. Children become bored, fidgety and sleepy. Even adults need to take a break from daily activities to recharge and build new energy for clear thinking. Likewise, as an employee, taking a mental health day from your job is very important to you and the proper functioning of any organization. And never let anyone talk you out of taking time off. Everyone should know when their bodies and minds are in distress. You wouldn't want to have the riot act read to you instead of being shown sympathy; if in your tired state you should send an email complaining about the boss and the boss' management style to the boss instead of your colleague. You also wouldn't want to work and push yourself until you pass out at your desk. As sad as it may be, the reality is that someone will be placed in your spot sooner than expected as if you didn't even exist. My father always told me that no one is indispensable. They can replace you in a heartbeat. So be wise and work smart.

Saying: All work and no play makes Jack a dull boy.

Is there always reward in working?

I recall the nursery rhyme, *Little Tommy Tucker Sings For His Supper.* Whether or not Tommy was working for his supper, the fact remains he was using up energy. Work is work! It's a matter of survival in some cases. People work to be paid. Some work yet they never get paid. They are *Ally Button who works for nothing*, according to the expression. And even if work is strenuous or not, over time the effects from it will leave you zapped, drained, tired and confused. Sports, greed, social activities, cleaning the house, sweeping the streets, farming, cooking, building construction, caring for the ill, relationships, driving a vehicle and flying a plane are all activities that can wear you out.

Also, believe it or not, sexual intercourse is no exception. It's hard work. Like a contortionist's role: twisting and turning, flipping back and forth, bend and touch toes, stand, squat, pushups and more. When all's done you look and feel as if Samson, the strongest man according to the bible, has whooped your ass. However, the good thing about having sex is that while you anticipate the hallelujah moment during the twists and turns, it allows you to burn calories. A maverick plan for those looking to lose unwanted pounds with a special touch. Inasmuch as the method is ideal for losing weight, females disappointed with their relationships will quickly let it be known they would rather keep the weight than take part in sexual activities. They remain operose with the idea: *it's better to rust than to wear*.

Why rust?! Whenever things take on a corrosive quality, the propensity for it to fall apart from the slightest move or touch could be devastating. Supple limbs are important to the human body. Likewise, greasing and oiling the bearings in a vehicle is very important for good functioning. What then will become of the people who willfully place themselves in a state of disuse atrophy? Besides the telltale signs of ageing, the only other atrophy that is pleasing and rewarding is a sweet tasting prune or raisin. What's better than an oxytocin moment? Don't do harm to yourselves if there is no just reward in what you are doing.

*Saying: Ebry day a fishin day but ebry day a
nuh fi kech fish.*
*Translation: Every day is fishing day but not
everyday is a day to catch fish.*
*Meaning: Some days there is no reward in
labor.*

Who can you trust to listen to your concerns?

*When your friend becomes your foes, into the
world your secrets go.* I grew up hearing this
phrase which still remains with me to this day. I
would be awashed with embarrassment if I
confided in someone about something
personal and then found out sometime later
that it did not remain with that person. Not only
would I be embarrassed but I would throw all
the unkind words and expletives at that
individual until I feel satisfied. I abhor
confrontation so I would blow all my anger
away from the culprit's hearing. The next move
would be to cut the buddy relationship between
us but still say, *good morning*, *good afternoon*
and *good evening*. According to the people of

old, *howdy and tenky nuh bruk noh square*. In other words continue to display good manners. No one can fistfight you for having good manners.

I remember back in the day when a child talked too much, an elder would refer to the child's mouth as being set on hinges. At another time the adage, *chatty chatty child always pay their parents' debt*, would be used. Today on the street a person who talks incessantly or releases information private or otherwise is referred to as someone *suffering from verbal diarrhea* or labeled a snitch. People's bad habits often impede progress among others. It's never a good thing neither is it acceptable to repeat things said in confidence to anyone. Once shared, the thought of being mocked, scorned and laughed at by friends, strangers and family weighs heavily on the person who has been let down by a dear friend.

It's wise to go easy with people when they engage you with something special for safe keeping. It's hard to detect when they are in a dismal and delicate place in daily and domestic living. An example would be someone who has seen numerous failures instead of success or is burdened with an illness to the point where evil thoughts are being conjured. It's not a secret that society can be harsh and judgmental when it comes to illnesses even when they are not caused through careless actions or behaviors. Good foods when handled in a bad and careless manner can cause illnesses and death too. Hence, educating people at the community level, on conduct, is necessary. They will become better citizens: Act responsible. Be great listeners. Show compassion. Be kind. Be respectful. Be trustworthy.

Saying: Ebry bess fren hab a bess fren.
Translation: Every best friend has a best friend.
Meaning: The person you take for your best friend also has a best friend.

Do you take your troubles to God?

It's up to everyone to determine who God is. Religion is a touchy subject, controversal.

Well, HELLO, this paragraph is not to win or determine souls neither religion. Every man to his own accord. I am familiar with the instruction: It's safe to take your woes and stories to God in prayer. But my opinion is, this would have to be a silent prayer because the fear exists that someone could hear you praying and then maliciously spread your business all over the place. Or, make a poster of all that was prayed and place it on a lamp post at a crosswalk somewhere in New York City. And in a world where social media exists, you will be mocked and talked about. *Your goose will be cooked*, according to the saying. The entire world will know and hear about you and your problems in a jiffy.

Watch out for the surrounding walls too when you pray alone and aloud because the proverbial saying, *walls have ears*, could be very true. Someone could be behind them in that opportune moment. However, in time you will have to decide on what to do about your problems. Ignore people and seek the proper help that you need. There is no disgrace in asking for help. Mean-spirited people love misery. Tune them out. It's difficult to do but at least try. Sing a lively song. Dance! Try with all your might to get out of the miry clay: your troubles. Delay is danger. *A stitch in time saves nine*. Seek Help! Life is precious. Live it! And live it healthy.

Saying: Nuh matta how boar hog hide undah sheep wool, him grunt betray him.
Translation: It doesn't matter how much the boar hog conceals itself in sheep's wool, it will be betrayed by its grunt.
Meaning: People's true behavior will always be revealed.

Are you a silent speaker?

Often times it has been said that actions speak louder than words. If you are an observant person, you will know when someone is trying to avoid you, give you the cold shoulder. When this happens, it would be a waste of time to question the person's behavior. Some people may object to this and call for a dialogue. What dialogue? The understanding is: When people toot their horn telling you to get out of the way, they mean get out of the way. Don't try to approach them because there may very well be a head on collision. Get out of their way. Not every signal should be questioned.

Overall body language is a kicker. It can let you down when you go about important businesses especially on a job interview if you are not in the know-how. Project yourself to suit. For example, one has to sit in a certain manner, make eye contact with the interviewer, fold hands in a certain manner, don't hug cheeks or cup hands in chin. Don't break wind no matter how nervous you are. If you have to, be sure to stifle it with a loud cough. The actions you exhibit at a job interview can determine your chance of being hired.

People speak different parts of their bodies. The feet are handy for a downpayment on sexual romps: playing footsie at the dinner table. Some people use their elbows to nudge the person beside them which serves as a hint to focus on something that requires attention, shut up or keep quiet. Most amusing are Jamaicans like myself who sometimes use our mouths to point at someone, something or place. The eyes, however are the most used when it comes to silent speaking. The language is piercing. In bygone days elders used their eyes to reprimand unruly children. They found it more effective and convenient than their voices in most cases. For example, when in public with a stubborn child, it's best to do the silent speaking. No parent would want to be ostracized for hitting a child in public. Hence, all it took to have unruly children cowering was a stare from parents or any adult. Isn't that amazing?! One big wide stare to instill manners and cease rowdy behavior.

I hardly believe an adult staring at a child to keep him or her in check still has honor. The 21st century has brought frightening changes and behaviors. Children are too busy being best friends with parents and in doing so it's very difficult for parents to draw a line of discipline when it comes time to do so. Back in the day children who went out of line with their parents would be reminded of the commandment which states: *children should honor their parents so that their days may be long on the land.* Today it's a different story as children ignore it and choose to argue, curse and get into physical altercations with their parents. As if that isn't enough, they back it up with: *parents should not provoke their children to wrath*, according to the bible. I recall a little girl who always said, *parents should not provoke their children to rass*. In her head the curse word *rass* was what she heard and not *wrath*. Children always get their words twisted until they know better. There is one thing I can say for sure and that is: an old time parent not giving interest in what the bible has to say would have asked an impertinent child, *Who is the parent. You or me*? In other words a child should behave like a child. Be obedient and respectful.

Saying: Play wid puppy, puppy lick yuh mouth. Play wid big dawg, big dawg bite yuh. Translation: Play with puppy, puppy licks your mouth. Play with big dog, big dog bites you. Meaning: Familiarity breeds contempt.

Are you cautious?

There is a feeling in our society that everyone is under a spectrum of some sorts. Big brother is watching. And just in case you believe that Big Brother is the *One above, namely the Heavenly Father*, you are in for a rude awakening when you find out it's technology. One such technology is the camera in an inquisitive role, which is dubbed eyes-in-the-sky. It has teamed up video traits. Movements! It is a device which is driving people crazy while teaching them to be more cautious in their goings, comings and actions.

I can only imagine how difficult it has become for the male who had the habit of standing against a light post, a tree, a wall or a parked vehicle to relieve himself of pee. They will have to find a new pee house or recycle a water bottle as pee pot. Some men are discreet using it. They sit in vehicles like little angels, looking out the window with focus on peeing. And, as for the nose pickers and spitters. Just when they think it's safe to dig their noses and flick pieces of crust and cough up phlegm and spit anywhere, a camera could be watching their sinister attack on public health.

When it comes to criminal activities, there seem to be no way out for the culprits as cameras capture them in their crooked, biased, atrocious, willful and wanton ways. It is amazing, surprising and rewarding to see how advanced the world has become in watching the movements of humans. The upgrade went from mirrors to video cameras in the most unlikely places. So be on your best behavior.

Saying: *It's better to be safe than sorry.*

How are your coping skills fairing as the world turns and heaves its underwear?

In days gone by the elders in my village used to warn children against airing their dirty linen in public. We had to be on our Ps and Qs at all times when in public. Show our best behavior. Be kind. Speak kindly of others, even in the face of our adversaries. Conceivably, there are factors and situations in our society with the disposition to create an air of uneasiness and discontent. A mini checklist would be: jobs, poverty, family, bosses, colleagues, party politics, foods, clothing, healthcare system, transportation and relationships.

However, none blows people's minds as much as 21st century party politics. Its rambo style has changed the climate and landscape of existence more than religion and sex had ever done. Laws from the beginning of time are surprisingly vulnerable. They do not hold firm as they should. The same goes for trust and loyalty. Because as greed and evil penetrate the minds of people, cunning attitudes take over. And whether or not society is in the mood, it's charted to receive daily screws from people drunk on power. They override principles and good judgement with their own set of rules, beliefs, personal grudges, feelings, revenge and self-interests. Not even a teflon condom is capable of saving society from being pregnant with worry and concern. The elders back in the day observing difficult situations would have said, *only salvation lasts forever, and it had better be the good one.*

Saying: *Day longa dan rope.*

Translation: *Day longer than rope.*
Meaning: *Time will right all injustices.*

Are you about to go out of your mind because of people's behavior?

With all the baleful, bilious, noxious and dissolute behavior floating about anyone can become a victim of poor health. Conduct at home and in the workplace is no different from the principles of party politics or politricks as labeled in the streets. Parents, children, friends, colleagues and bosses who stick to your butts like diapers often ignore values such as: honesty, fairness, truthfulness. They have no reservations when it comes to embracing fame and doing things against guidelines and policies to irritate you and make you seem useless. The idea is to hold oneself responsible for all the wrongs. But do not be too quick to blame oneself because sometimes people have serious issues and instead of seeking help they will quickly identify someone to be their beating post.

It would be unfair not to mention that some individuals can be brutes, brats and bitches, BBB. They will drag their domestic life along with them wherever they go. They even take it to their houses of worship. They feel more secure bullying others instead of addressing their personal problems. As for those little mamas' and papas' angels. Otherwise known as brats and pets. Whenever they are faced with a professional awakening, it's showtime because they don't know how to separate the real world from their home life. Their only recourse is to run in an office and slam doors or bang on desks, push the chairs around noisily, scream fuck, I hate you, I quit or even cry as if someone is beating them with a pestle. If Granny should take a look at this paragraph her advice to victims of people's bad behavior would be: *The darkest part of the night is just before dawn*. Be encouraged.

Saying: *Duppy know who fi friten.*
Translation: *Duppy knows who to frighten.*
Meaning: *Bullies pick on those who are vulnerable.*

Are incentives great encouragers?

Money makes the mare gallop! It's a beauty to see the horses run at the Kentucky Derby or any given day at the race tracks. But before they run, customers have to place bets on their favorite horse or the one that is most likely to win. The horses cannot run until bets have been placed. Likewise, in our society people who perform well in whatever they choose to do should be rewarded.

People placed in charge of others should avoid being biased when dishing out rewards. No *curry favor or kisses by favor* should be expressed. Impart praise to people who present high quality performance, regardless of color, creed, physical appearance or looks. Or, even when they are not so good, give a word of encouragement to boost them.
Encouragement sweetens labor is the belief of the old. Even in intimate relationships men will step up their game, be nice when they know that sex is promised to them. They will go above and beyond to please their eye candy until that promised time arrives. So get all you can out of them while they wait for the frivolous

torpedo moment, in bed, vehicle, under a pimento tree, the beach or elsewhere. Luck comes in all forms not only with the lotteries. Milk those men for all they are worth. You could end up with a new car or a downpayment on a house. Let the encounter be worthwhile when men are in a state of sweet temporary insanity.

Please note that I am not encouraging anyone to indulge in robbery or unpleasant behavior. But if I should listen to the wisdom of the wise old ladies on dealing with men, one of the thoughts to remember would be: *a man's heart is soft during an erection and when there is no erection his heart is hard.* Not only that, the wise old ladies also claim that a woman is always on the receiving end. Take that any way you want.

Saying: *When jackass sumell corn him gallop.*
Translation: *When the jackass smells corn it gallops.*
Meaning: *Use the appropriate encouragement for each person.*

Can smart people do the wrong things?

There are people in high places, smart people, who are faced with problems and in trying to fix them they will resort to callous and unscrupulous behavior. They abuse the use of power, engage in sordid deals, commit fraud and more. One would think that smart people focus on great ideas and do things that are acceptable to see them through their dilemma. There was a time in society when people would seek individuals who dealt in "grease palm". In other words they are people who love when they are being paid hefty sums of money to get things done the illegal way. Such behavior often comes back to haunt the individuals who are involved. A mistake will be made. Or, some jealous or envious person will make a report to the relevant authorities about those individuals illicit way to acquire money. In the end the entire lot, stock and barrel will be penalized. Jailed in some situations.

The stalwart christians of old always advised others that if they would like to see God's face; It's best to do things the right and proper way instead of being caught in a tangled web that can demolish your character. Truthfully, those christians always inject the holy fear in me as a child. I feared them as much as I had feared the name God. I deprived myself of all the most wanted youthful kisses because they said God is always watching over us. Little did I know it was conscience, good judgement and decision.

Overall, when people are faced with difficulty or in a predicament, they will do what had seemed impossible to them to remedy the situation. An appropriate adage in Jamaican dialect would be: *when trouble tek yuh pickney shut fit yuh* (forcing yourself into a child's clothes). And rightly so, because should night turn to day, it's guaranteed that people would be caught in all kinds of uncompromising positions and situations. For example, not every prostitute is a prostitute at heart. Or, not every go-go dancer is a go-go at heart. People do odd jobs to pay their rent, tuition, mortgages and more. Every heart knows its own sorrow. The extra jobs they do are to make ends meet, stay on top of their finances. My granny would have said, *circumstances cause jackass to wear braces*. Or, *circumstances alter cases.*

Saying: *Hungry mek monkey blow fire.*
Translation: *Hunger caused the monkey to blow fire.*
Meaning: *People do the impossible when it becomes necessary.*

Are you giving yourself good grades?

It's always best to document your achievements in all you do. Do not leave it up to anyone to do it for you. Keep score cards or charts on your failures and successes. See what outweighs the other and when you are satisfied, pinpoint and show others how efficient you are. By the same token speak about your failures and shortcomings. But by a long shot, don't undersell yourself just to please others because you fear them thinking that self-praise is no recommendation. Blow your own horn when you have to. Let people around the bend know that you are coming. It's a different world now. Speak up! One popular New York Mayor, Ed Koch, during his tenure, used to ask the question, *How am I doing*? I was always tickled and impressed by his boldness and awareness. He believed in feedback which some people will see as opening the door to criticism. When that becomes necessary, tell yourself that there are constructive criticisms. The good will always outweigh the bad. No need to worry.

One of my sisters once said that if she was handed three prizes to give away, the first prize would go to herself, the second prize to herself and the third prize to herself. All three prizes would go to herself. In this situation you may bitch about her being dishonest, arrogant and selfish. But before you do, why don't you try giving yourself prizes too and see how you feel about it? Know your ultimate account on receiving three prizes and most importantly how it feels to be nominated three times and in the top three spots by no one other than yourself. I used to hear the elders say: *Parson always krissen (baptize or bless) his pickney/child first*. In other words, Parson handles his business first before assisting others.

Saying: *Jankro tink im pickney white.*

Translation: *John Crow thinks its child is white.*
Meaning: *Everyone thinks highly of what they own.*

What is your radar detecting?

Change is a good thing. We all yearn for change at some point in life. Sometimes change happens to us without us being aware of it. A friend or bickering people will notice that you no longer share your mangoes and avocados in the manner you used to. Your spouse may notice that lovemaking is not like it used to be. You may be invited by the friend to join in a conversation about the change in you. But in the end you decide to take offence or even hold malice against your friend instead of bickering people. Because in your mind it's all nonsense that your friend is telling you. The friend's only interest is to stir trouble. A defensive behavior is not an unusual response. But one thing you should know is that *standing in a forest doesn't allow you to see the tallest tree in it.* You will have to step outside of the forest to see it.

To alleviate malice among good friends and stop bickering people in their tracks, it's always a good thing to give yourself spot checks. Random checks like the policemen who hide in bushes or by the wayside to check if drivers have their proper credentials for driving or if their vehicles are properly licensed. Sometimes you will be amazed by the findings of random checks. Don't be afraid to ask others to give you their honest opinions about your development or you as an individual. Get your random check. Unknown to you, you could be swerving erratically in your path to the edge of a precipice.

Saying: Clothes nuh cover up character.
Translation: Clothes do not cover up character.
Meaning: Actions speak louder than words.

Should I focus on taking care of others before myself?

For some people the self is always out of the picture. Others constantly come before oneself.

Of course it's great to think and care about others but in order to do so effectively, one has to be in good condition. Do not become too busy or absorbed in the diatribes that are taking place in the world. All kinds of gossips exist. *Gossip should be put to good use.* But don't be in a hurry to listen to malicious gossip. I pause to give thanks to the long gone elders of Maidstone and the surrounding villages, Manchester, Jamaica, on their wisdom and especially the lady who had shared her opinion: *Gossip should be put to good use.* Gossip comes with lessons but unfortunately they are seen for what they are, gossip.

Focusing on gossip too is almost the same as putting others before self. Set the distraction aside. Find time to listen to yourself. Hear yourself out; don't set the self aside. Know when it's doing overtime, running out of energy. Feeding the body, mind and soul with things that are comforting and uplifting are important. Go dancing. Listen to music. Go see a movie. Go on a nature walk. Above all, love self first. Do things that excite you and make you shout for joy. Sound the alarm of an orgasm, fake and real. That certainly would be hinting to others in close proximity that you are taking great care of yourself. You are a winner!

Saying: Charity begins at home.
Meaning: Loving self first will lead you to love others.

Are you destructive?

I recall when mischievous children used the latrine walls at my elementary school as a billboard. They defaced it with all kinds of school work; from arithmetic to the popular transcription *The quick brown fox jumped over the lazy dogs*. Everyday, in the classroom, this sentence was written in cursive to cultivate good penmanship. And quite noticeably it carried all the letters of the alphabet. Unfortunately, there were times when slackness and loose language prevailed on those latrine walls, giving little thought to the transcription. The most stressful thing is that the culprit or possible culprits who defaced those walls with expressions such as *pussy is good for man or crab louse can jump 10 feet high*, were never caught. Hence, the good students had to suffer for the bad ones, or wall abusers, by cleaning away the smut. Our desks were no exception when it comes to tidiness. We had to sandpaper away spilled inks and any little signs of hard use to make them look new and beautiful again.

Likewise, outside of school, there were mischievous children who wrote "please clean me" on motor vehicles that were covered with dust. The adults called the children's actions rude. Some even referred to them as street urchins and idlers who have no regard and respect for people's property. Today their actions would be considered graffiti, which carries penalties and punishment in some countries. So the wise word would be, be careful where you write your feelings. Do not deface properties that do not belong to you. Be respectful.

If the need to express yourself is urgent, write whatever is bothering you in the sand and then erase it with your feet. Or, write it on a piece of paper, read it aloud to yourself, rip it into tiny pieces and then toss it to the wind or burn it. Send it off with a strong statement or an adjective which gives satisfaction. And should anyone see you and comment that your sins are catching up with you, please count to ten in your mind because such a statement could possibly ignite World War III. Also, bear in mind that a layman's advice may be poignant but not as much as the advice from a professional. One who is lettered in the field of counseling. Don't go through your crisis alone.

Saying: Yuh pred yuh bed hawd, yuh haffi li dung pan it it hawd.
Translation: You spread your bed hard, you must lie on a hard bed.
Meaning: You reap what you sow.

Are you a procrastinator?

I have heard the saying that *procrastination is the thief of time* umpteen times more than the shortest bible verse: *Jesus wept*. Parents have good eyes. Meaning that they can notice unusual signs and behaviors in their children. They know when their children have become lackadaisical, tardy and drag their feet in doing things. Often times they blame the conditions on worms wreaking havoc in the children's intestines, which called for a dose of herb medicine to be administered to each child. It was imperative. Parents always run their medical duty in the wee hours of the morning, by surprise to erase fear and crying. But no matter how they tried to avoid the behavior, some children always try to escape under the beds or bawl murder. In the end it would have been a useless effort for the children because parents always win. Medicine served because procrastination wasn't a game to them.

My father in one of his teachable moments about life had told me about a man who visited a neighbor, early one morning, to borrow his donkey. On arriving, he decided to exercise good manners, not appear as a user or burden. So he engaged in small talks with the donkey owner. During the course of their conversations another neighbor stopped by and after greeting the two men, he turned to the owner of the donkey and asked if he could borrow his donkey. The owner gladly told him he could and added that there was no need to bring back the donkey in a hurry.

The neighbor who was first on the scene to borrow the donkey sighed, wiping away sweat. He then looked at the donkey owner and said, *Do you know that my main intention this morning was to borrow the donkey*? The donkey owner not lending any sympathy to the dilly-dallying borrower looked at him and said, *You damn idiot! Look how much time you wasted chatting instead of stating the true purpose of your visit!*

Saying: Don't beat around the bush
Meaning: Be frank.

Are you putting yourself in harms way?

There is no doubt that a person's behavior can be influenced by his or her environment or circle of friends. Social media is one of the avenues that has the power to condition individuals too. And given the political climate, on social media it's difficult not to get caught in the blizzard of bullies, information and comments amounting to toxins and free radicals. From twitter to Facebook to Instagram and more it is expected that a poison dart could be hurled at any given moment.

People without voices and who were less likely to give their opinion have at times morphed into fiends of some sorts on social media. All inhibitions have been removed because there is no physical appearance. The technology allows bloggers to feel comfortable. They will advance into super hyped comments, especially when trolls get to work with their biohazard fingers and minds. Even the righteous ones who are there on social media to view only, keep the peace and drive away the spirit of lucifer, will also find out that they are no match for the atheists, people of various denominations and those who are driven by their ancestors.

In my opinion, when it comes to social media, it's imperative to clothe minds with hazmat materials such as humor, blind eyes, silence and respect to ward off unkind words and behavior. Make no bones about it, the electronic world is comparable to the physical world. Ruffians and hooligans live there. So it's of great significance and value to stop and breathe and detox. Go on a fast. Return to view social media with fresh eyes. Pay less attention to the people who provide a diet of hateful words and rhetoric which have the capability to adhere to the mind like leeches and distort one's inner peace.

Saying: Nuh mattah how cockroach drunk, him nah walk pass fowl yawd.
Translation: It doesn't matter how drunk cockroach is, he knows not to walk pass fowl's yard.
Meaning: Be aware of your surroundings and operations.

Is peer pressure toxic?

Peer pressure is an awful zone to be caught up in. It has the propensity to lead people down the tubes of destruction. Pause and scream if you have to. Take deep breaths and then exhale. Let it be known that peer pressure is real. One of the aspects of peer pressure is that it often inveigles you to live above your means. It persuades you to desire things that make you feel uncomfortable. For example stealing money to buy a pair of name brand sneakers or topnotch designer clothing. You will do all of that just to be in the swing of things. To feel accepted by your peers and to impress others. But have you ever considered what will become of you when you are pressured into upgrading your stealing habits to get even more pricer items? Chances are you will end up in prison.

If you find that you are doing things against your values, please speak with someone who can help you to get back on track. Bad habits are not copacetic! Get out of that zone as fast as you can.

Saying: If yuh si everybody a run tek time.
Translation: If you see everybody running, take your time.
Meaning: Don't be too eager to follow others.

Is a tattletale readily accepted at home?

Usually when people decide to tattle they are influenced by fear, acquisitiveness, envy, jealousy, insecurity, wants and hatred. The practice occurs among siblings more than anyone would want to see or know about. Some people will refer to those children as fussy or unhappy. And if we look hard at the behavior there is always a huge reason. For example, a parent might favor one child over the other because of their physical appearance, complexion, academics and athletic ability.

Back in the day such a child was mischievously labeled as the *grand-prize* by observant people outside of the family. And God forbid if the child who receives less attention should see the esteemed child taking sugar or a cookie from the cupboard at home without permission. It would be a polaroid or sweepstakes moment to the less favored child as he or she reports to the parents on the looming bad habit of the child that is cherished by them. Under such circumstances, good parenting will call for a reprimand or some type of punishment to be imposed on the child who took the sugar and cookie without permission.

Overall, at home, complaints lodged to parents by any child required proof. If not the complaints are denounced and dismissed, and the child viewed as stirring trouble or being cantankerous.

Saying: Ben di tree wen it young; wen it old it wi bruk.
Translation: Bend the tree when it's young; it will break when it's old.
Meaning: It is easier to train children when they are young than when they are older.

Should a tattletale be given honor in the workplace?

Everywhere, modern changes by way of technology have infringed on the usual way of office procedures and have opened up a crater to accommodate tattletales. A person who tattles expects benefits. Perhaps a promotion or salary increase. Such illicit behavior spreads commotion and disunity among workers. The work atmosphere becomes toxic and production wanes as employees walk about the office giving each other evil looks. At some point in our lives, if we are honest, we can say that we have put up resistance to change and not as much to the individuals who tattle.

The process to acquire change is hectic and more so when the blind is leading the blind. Compared to tattling which takes very little effort because the person behind it is usually an expert. Before change happens, a good assessment of the old should be looked at along with the new and if feasible take the plunge. The old adage, *New broom sweeps clean but old broom knows corners*, should stand as a mantra in any line of change. Be it at home, work or play.

Not all modern changes stand firm. They are weak just like the new buildings that are being constructed these days. Certainly not solid like the buildings from a hundred years. Inasmuch as they have no substance, structural traits and charm, the builders' intentions are to dazzle our eyes with fancy embellishment to pull us in. But rest assured when mother nature is in its wrath we will find out that they are made with mediocre materials. Shim sham beauties done with greed and no durability. When I think about the modern buildings there is one popular Jamaican dancehall song that comes to mind: *Pretty Face and Bad Character*, sung by Chaka Demus.

If change can fail so does tattling in the workplace. Blabbermouths are unhappy and insecure creatures. Maybe as a rule all blabbermouths should be given a pacifier. This will encourage them not to speak if there is nothing positive to say. A competent manager should know when to listen. A competent manager should know when tattling is useful and is in the best interest of the company. Wouldn't it be better to tattle on the person who wastes workplace sundries than the person who makes numerous swift visits to the restroom? Common sense should tell the person who loves to tattle that the numerous swift visits would be to release wind and not to squeeze love bumps seen on faces, waste time or dodge work.

The person who tattles often in the workplace will eventually develop a chronic imaginary behavior. They will make up stories about others to keep the gullible managers excited and busy *giving the talk*. Those who are victims will feel embarrassed and insulted. And not to mention those with fragile egos. They will quit their jobs or perhaps become a basket case: uninterested in work and seek medical attention for stress and depression. They may even feel harassed and file complaints and lawsuits. And heaven helps everyone if, because of a sassy tattletale, a worker is pushed to the point where they become disgruntled. It is no secret that disgruntled people have a funny way of wiping out creation. Old time people had a brilliant way to quell situations or make peace. They used adages. One of my favorite ones that would suit a tattletale is: *Tan an si nuh spwile noh dance; a intahferance mash it up*. Which means people should mind their own business. Do not insert yourself to stir trouble.

Saying: No mek one donkey choke yuh.
Translation: Do not allow one donkey to choke you.

Meaning: Do not be misled by a fool.

Should a team member be allowed to do the work of a manager?

As a child I was assigned chores at home. However, there were times when laziness took charge of my body and a deal would be made with one of my siblings to do the work. Giving up one of my dumplings was the favored form of payment. And I had better stick with the plan or I would be bullied into paying up. The concept used at home is no different from what takes place on the outside. Caution is necessary though because some tasks, in the workplace especially a medical facility, should be for certain eyes only and not subordinates. It's imperative that managers should have limits and boundaries on the work that subordinates should assist them with. Team members should offer to help, but not be forced to do so. Bullies are not welcome in the workplace.

A well-prepared manager is expected to find time to oversee and observe how each worker is handling the tasks that they are assigned. A manager should not be of the opinion that their purpose in the workplace is to only delegate work. Many hands make the work lighter. A manager should know all aspects of the work and procedures so that they can help when there is an emergency. A manager should not supervise a worker if they have no knowledge of how the work is done. Also, the onus should be on a manager to be at work on time to take note of the employees who are tardy and the ones who are leaving before their scheduled time. It is neither fair nor professional to rely on or put such a burden on any team member whether or not they are the manager's pet. A manager should not be of a conniving nature. A manager should not abuse the strength of a team member for their convenience and personal climb in an organization. Control should be in the team member's court as well as the manager's. Work with balance not in tiers.

Saying: Every tub ha fi sit on its own bottom.

Translation: Every tub has to sit on its own bottom.
Meaning: Every person is responsible for their actions and welfare.

Have you been overlooked for a job that you had an interest in?

People go to school with the intention of equipping themselves with the knowledge that would land them in their dream jobs. Unfortunately, the job market is not as illustrious as it used to be. There are more dogs than bones. The job pickings are few. Modern technology has bullied job seekers into bemoaning the fact of going to school to get an education to better their lives. I am sure that if some job seekers had the wherewithal of situations they would punch the heck out of all robots, spilling all their electrical fandangles, accoutrements and microchips like minced meat.

Sometimes with reluctant hope, job seekers are taking whatever they can get until they get what they want. They will remain at the bottom of the totem pole in a company until the opportunity presents itself to move up to a higher position. And sometimes even if they are qualified they are denied the position on various grounds such as not having required tenure, skills and seniority. Sometimes people looking to climb the ladder of success in a company will find out that academic ability is not the sole criterion to land them in a prestigious position. Manners, attire and deportment are looked into to make a decision.

However, it would be disappointing to hear that a person is denied a job offer because they do not *fit the mold.* Rumors in the street have it that *fitting the mold* is the latest hex phrase used by the hiring staff in some places. It would be of interest to find out who gave them the mold and what does it constitute. Until then, it's befitting to say that incompetent people always make others wonder, feel ashamed and insecure; yet they remain in control.

Saying: Wen plantin waan dead it shoot.

Translation: When plantain wants to die it shoots.
Meaning: When people are not concerned about the good preservation of job and others, they act stupidly.

Are you taking on more work than you can manage?

To be competent is an excellent trait and skill. And this works best for anyone who has a paying job. Unfortunately, when you are competent work gets dumped on you. Gradually you become inundated and overwhelmed. Yet remain in silence because you are held in high esteem by your bosses and company. In the meantime your behavior can lead to chaos and constipate the workflow. Big hold up! When discovered, no one will remember how competent you are and the chance of you being fired is likely. You outdid yourself trying to impress them instead of expressing that you cannot handle any additional work until you have completed the tasks at hand. All that could have been avoided if you had been true to yourself, your manager/boss and to your colleagues. Hence, blame yourself for any consequences you may face.

Don't be a spoiler in the workplace because you want to show that you are competent. Your competence could become precedence. And how many people are capable of living up to an expectation that hasn't been given an overall test. No one wants to see the workflow constipated. It creates moans and groans. Stay with quality not volume to drive you sick. Handle your work in such a manner that things flow freely. Never take on more than you can manage. In my Jamaican tongue, even jankro (john crow) the scavenger, a creature in nature that flies around, knows how to handle its business. According to the elders, *jankro noh how it bottom stay that's why it nuh swallow abbey seed*. In other words, the john crow is not taking up what it cannot manage. The word on the street is that it passes its waste through the mouth because it has no anus. To be truthful, I am frightened by the knowledge of old time people, especially those without higher education. They knew things intuitively in their own way that now correlate to the modern workplace.

Saying: Craven choke puppy dog.
Meaning: Do not bite off more than you can chew.

When last have you had a conversation with yourself?

Bad behavior and bad manners are springing up here, there and everywhere. They must be the latest fad. If that is the situation, I readily decline because as a child my parents told me that good conduct and manners will take me anywhere in the world. Not only that but I would blossom into a beautiful young lady. Those old time people had a way to butter up children which helped them to feel good about themselves, especially the ones who conjured evil and morbid thoughts.

Sadly, the twenty first century has advanced with some people exhibiting volatile behavior. The latest social correctness to address the situation is labeled, "it's time to have a conversation".

But how can we have a conversation if we have not visited and chatted with oneself first. In today's world, unless you are not obviously wearing an earphone or bluetooth, you will be viewed as a crazy person for talking to yourself. You could also be conceived as hearing voices in your head. Or, perhaps someone might suggest that you are high on drugs; from Molly, to crack to cocaine, to heroin to ganja. Or, in the name of refinement for the higher ups, it would be opioids. The subtle approach among some people in society is disgusting. Aren't they aware that all drugs can be deadly even when they are supposed to do good? The effect of drugs hardly ever discriminate.

At home, my mother used to talk with herself while she did chores. Her behavior even solicited her own laughs. Sometimes I would hear her laughing and saying, *But a wah duh him* (What's the matter with him)? In Jamaican dialect "him" can be unisex. So, I told myself that she was talking to herself about my father.

One thing for sure, I knew that my mother was not crazy. She functioned like a normal mother around the house. She took care of the family and kept us well fed, clean and grounded. Now that I am an adult, I sometimes find myself doing what my mother used to do. A monologue in which I laugh, talk, ask myself questions about me, reprimand self, and damn and blast anything that is bothering me in a loud manner. Devil! Go to the pit of hell where you belong! Don't mess with me! Go!

The fact of the matter is when it comes to the devil, *it's monkey see monkey do*. People in their moment always let the devil have the brunt of it. Honesty matters to me most though, when I am in a deliberate zone with myself. I will hug myself. I will stand before the mirror and then throw a kiss at the figure I see in the mirror. Make eye contact with that figure and say: I love you! You are beautiful! You are smart! You are such a looker! I garnish myself with all the wonderful accolades. I am sure that there are people who pat themselves and treat themselves to something fancy and delicious when they are doing great; or even on their down days and sad days. Some may pinch themselves hard if they are at fault and in that moment will make a pledge to do better. However, if it is identified that situations and concerns are unmanageable there is always the option to seek proper and professional help. Don't do it by yourself. Hallucination and paranoia avenues, deep bend, on the edge and on the verge of jumping from a high place are not places where anyone would want to be. Know the signs. Get the help you need. Go have a conversation with someone.

Saying: Be true to yourself.

Are you a giver?

The more you give, the more you will receive is an encouraging statement. Do you believe this? As far as I am concerned such a statement was more believable back in the day. For example a farmer with excess produce or even without the excess would share his crop free of cost. Today this doesn't happen as often. Everyone is about money whether or not they know the value. It has become a habit among some people in our society to sell everything even when they steal it. The motto on the street is *nothing for nothing and very little for your money*.

If you are a giver and you are not replenishing your source, please note that one day it will diminish...depleted. Done! You will end up with the shudda cudda talk and your thoughts fixed on the wise old saying, *Yuh gi weh yuh ass an a shit chue yuh ribs.* To translate: You gave away your ass and is shitting through your ribs. Meaning: You sacrificed everything and left yourself stranded...without.

A giving person is always taken for an idiot or seen as a sucker for sad stories. And heaven help the giver who decides to cease operations. The moment it is made known, the giver will be labeled the worse person under the sun. Isn't it weird how the human mind sometimes crafts and sees things? Such a despondent way to behave. Yet some givers keep on giving. There is nothing that can stop them.

Saying: It's better to give than to receive.

Is it difficult to decline someone's offer?

Some people lack conscience when it comes to accepting offers. Even when something is offered to them out of politeness they just do not have it in them to refuse. Please learn that sometimes when people expose you to an offer, it doesn't always come from the heart. Ask for discernment when you are faced with an offer. If you are the kind of person who always goes to bed with wants and wakes up with gimme, you will be caught in a web of deceit.

Nine times out of ten, the person who makes the offer will be looking for something in return. An acquaintance was caught in that web of deceit. She thought it was a blessing when a male friend kept giving her money. Ultimately the blessing turned into a brouhaha when the friend looked at her neck and noticed that a *dracula* existed in her life. In the moment there is no doubt that he thought about the many kisses of ecstasy *count dracula* had planted at the neck and possible hidden areas of her body. Perhaps he could have gotten a bite too

if his intentions were not shady. Not try to bait
her with money at a vulnerable time.

*Saying: If yuh waan half a bread, beg
summady buy it. If yuh want whole a bread buy
it yuh self.*
*Translation: If you want a half loaf of bread ask
someone to buy it. If you want a whole loaf of
bread buy it yourself.*
Meaning: Do not abuse people's kindness.

Are you a taker?

Long ago, I learned not to take money or any
gifts from men because it always comes with a
hidden agenda even when it doesn't seem that
way. Thank goodness for strict parents. In my
village in Jamaica, my father was selected to
hand out farm work tickets to the men who
were interested in working on farms in the
United States of America. Anyone who
received the ticket had to pass a medical which
qualified them to go to America. One young
man, on his return, presented me with a heart
shaped wristwatch. I was shocked but happy

and quickly went to show it to my mother. My mother was of a light hue and I noticed her face turned almost cherry red. The signs of shock and anger revealed when she opened her mouth and asked me where I got the watch from. I trembled as I told her and without another word said, she invited me to come along with her to return the watch to the giver.

My mother scolded me the entire way, telling me that the giver will be wanting *something in return as soon as he goes around the corner*. What something was she talking about? I thought. I had nothing to give anyone. Perhaps she was talking about my favorite food, boiled flour dumpling. I was embarrassed to the point of holding my legs tight for pee not to escape, when my mother and I arrived at the young man's home and she told me to hand him back the watch. As I did so, she told him not to give me anything again. Not even the bible! The young man wiped sweat from his face, while he explained to her that he just wanted to show appreciation for my father's kind gesture. My mother having the last word told him to show the gesture to someone else who was his age. She even had the guts to mention to him that I hadn't even started to see what I am supposed to see and one way or the other no man is going to spoil her daughter. "I want no *belly* (pregnant child) in my home", she said, ordering me to go ahead of her as she left. My mother in her character depicted gale force winds when she sighted possible danger for her girls..

Saying: Dawg a sweat an long hair hide it.
Translation: Dog is sweating but its long hair is hiding it.
Meaning: Things are not always as they seem.

Is there comfort in being a liar?

Whenever I catch someone telling a lie, I am quick to remind them that it's easier to dodge a thief than a liar. People can go to prison for life because of a liar. As a child telling lies came with consequences. Standing before my parents and to have my lips pulled and twisted after being caught in a lie was painful and embarrassing. My lies were not enormous compared to politicians with their phantom promises. Yet I paid a price.

My lies were little things like pinching the bread, taking a little sugar, a biscuit or a cracker and denying that I did it. Or, saying that I did my chores when I didn't. I told lies at home, but never outside of it. My parents firmly believed that lying leads to thievery. They instilled good values in me. I practiced good habits at home so that I could take them with me anywhere I go. According to the saying, *I learned to dance at home before going abroad*. At my current age, I do not need to become the ultimate liar and crook which would land me in jail. If going to jail was in my plan I should be looking to come home now, not going.

Little lies and big lies. All lies are lies. There is no difference even when they are told in varying degrees: pathological liar, rass liar, fucking liar, stinking liar, convenient liar, religious liar or old liar. And may Jah grant comfort to the liars who shall face ridicule and have all kinds of labels placed on them according to their anatomy: bigfoot liar, big head liar, bang belly liar, long nose liar, wide nose liar, big mouth liar, big pussy liar and big wood liar, just to name a few. At the end of the day lying is not a wise choice. Speak truth, always.

Saying: Long run shawt kech.
Translation: Long run, short catch.
Meaning: It may take a long time for you to be apprehended for wrong doings, but one day you will be caught.

Do you have nimble hands?

The elders back in the day usually reprimand children about raising their hands to hit others. It didn't matter who was right or wrong, hitting was a dirty habit, an awful and unkind practice. According to the elders the aggressor could lose an arm if the victim got angry and retaliated. Adults taught children to speak to each other instead of hitting. "Yuh cyaan talk without hitting yuh one annada? Why oonu hand so nimble?", they would ask. If a girl struck a male, she would be told by the elders that it's wrong to hit men based on the fact that they will retaliate with the strength of hercules.

By the same token, when the boys were the culprit, the elders would tell them that little boys should not get into the habit of hitting girls because the behavior would become commonplace in adulthood.

The punishment given to a male for hitting females could have lasting effects. It's best that males and females use their hand to do worthwhile things. Keep hands humble not nimble. Humans are not punching bags. A strike on any part of the body could result in death or medical crisis. If tempers flare please talk with each other about the situation. Do not hit, strike or punch. The only punch that anyone should engage in a glass of fresh tropical fruit punch with a dash of a secret ingredient.

Saying: Wen plantain waan dead it shoot.
Translation: When plantain wants to die it shoots.
Meaning: When the plantains comes to perfection it is reaped and used. Likewise when people do not care about preserving the character of others they do stupid things.

Do you believe in generational curse?

Sometimes I wonder why I was born beautiful and not rich. And I bet a lot of you are saying the same thing or will use another statement. Weak finance is considered one of the top items when it comes to generational curses. Everyone could use extra money on any given day. Sometimes when I am not praying for extra money, or hoping for good luck with the lottery and daily numbers, I will raise my voice in singing the long ago hit song: *Money Money Money*, by The O'Jays, an American group. Some people will save and accumulate a decent amount of money whereas no matter how hard others try, they could never save not even a quattie. The scenario is: you have done well at school, graduated, found gainful employment and worked hard but for some reason you will find that you cannot meet your financial obligations. And it's not that you are living above your means. Sometimes the blame is placed on the excessive amount of taxes deducted from salaries. Such a situation perhaps has courted maternal calling several times. Keep a steady stream of young ones coming. Almost everything is taxed according to an elderly lady who once told me that she wouldn't be surprised if one day she heard that taxes have been imposed on the penis; a *pole tax*, she chuckled. Seasoned old ladies are fun. They keep things real.

Without a doubt, though, there are definitely some families who are successful in all that they do without even putting out much effort. They shine when it comes to education, marriage and businesses. One try and that's all it can take to turn everything into enormous wealth and happiness.

There is also the speculation that illnesses, atrocious behaviors, bad relationships and marriages are linked to generational curses. The weirdest speculation is that generational curses usually come from the male side of the family. If grandpa was an evil man, unfortunate events will occur in the generations after him. If he was a good man, goodness will flow through the generations after him. Perhaps there is an element of truth to the saying: *the good you do will live after you.*

Saying: Father suck the sour grapes and set the children's teeth on edge.

Meaning: It's difficult to escape the deeds of the father.

How often are derogatory labels placed on a female?

A female is often viewed as being promiscuous or labeled a whore should she choose to surround herself with many male friends. Labels have been placed on women ever since the bible story about Adam and Eve was made known. If I should address their garden story my way, Adam would have been arrested for lack of self control with his *snake*. Knowledge can be explored in many ways. And the more knowledge lends itself to us the clearer things become. We even become concerned and as such, since the turn of the 21st century, there is a hold up in referring to a female as beautiful, pretty, kind, loving, honest, motherly and decent. All the wonderful labels and accolades are not free flowing like they used to be. Are women dangerous or considered a threat?

Even by the stretch of my imagination I would not want to think that planet earth has been replaced by a planet of selfish individuals. I would rather conclude that things have changed course. The woman has made it known that her place is no longer in the kitchen. And her demand to have equal pay is legitimate. Because of her boldness she has warranted labels such as: damn bitch, wicked brute, money grabber, dog, low life, horse head and ugly fuck among others. Labels can be disheartening and unkind. As the world turns, there is hardly anything like brotherly and sisterly love. Every kind of situation chronicled, from melodramas to platonic relationships to woebegone ones to good deeds are linked to fuck. Are people wearing their pubic hair in the wrong place, the head, allowing it to impede good thinking?

In my lifetime I cannot count the amount of times that I have heard people say women and duppy (ghosts), bear the worst labels. Many stories have been told about ghosts dashing across people's path and destroying things. It's easy to blame the ghost for everything when people set out to achieve and end up failing because of their rancorous ways, approach and attitude. If it weren't for bad luck a woman and duppy wouldn't have any luck at all.

Saying: Everything bad weh happen in a sea a shark dweet.
Translation: Everything bad that has happened in the sea is blamed on the shark.
Meaning: Mischievous people always get blamed for others wrongdoings.

How often are derogatory labels placed on a male?

There is no denying that people have a way with labels when it comes to the male and especially when they have been hurt, upset or encounter a failed relationship. There are assigned labels such as: little dick so and so or long dick so and so, damn crook, dirty liar, and son of a bitch. Dirty liar is mostly affixed to a male who is caught having multiple affairs, especially one who is married and lead unsuspecting females to believe that he lives with his aunt or sister. Oh my goodness! Is there a sane and sober person around these days? Clearly the male gets a bad rap like the female when it comes to labels. It's an even-steven judgement for female and male. The elders would have said, *What is good for the goose is also good for the gander.*

The label *son of a bitch* makes me think. My mother had told me that *bitch* addresses the female dog. Aren't humans supposed to be the higher class of animals? I wouldn't want anyone to indirectly refer to my mother as a bitch by calling any of her sons, *son of a bitch.* But based on proper definition, the word bitch can also be used to describe a vulgar woman. I bet my mother knew that but chose to consider it a taboo word. Well, if she was around she would be surprised to hear that the word *bitch* has become a popular all purpose word. As an example, should a spoon fall to the ground while cooking, it would be labeled *damn bitch* before picking it up.

On that note, a relative mentioned that in life she learnt not to lament and show displeasure when things fall to the ground because the Lord knew beforehand that she needs exercise and to also release her inner spirit. The interesting part is that she sometimes grapples with the item on the ground numerous times using all kinds of labels before beguiling it with: *In the name of Jesus*, to get a good grasp and then return to the vertical position. This goes to show that some labels are not magical. They cause stress more than trying to put a square peg in a round hole.

Saying: Cause parrot mek nize dem seh a him one nyam banana.
Translation: Because the parrot is noisy, it is blamed for eating the banana.
Meaning: The loudest and most obvious always gets blamed.

Are you spiteful?

Children may appear and act innocent but they can be spiteful especially to their siblings. My childhood has the perfect blueprint. They put their plan into effect during mealtime at the dining table. For example, a sibling would shift focus to a make believe scorpion on the wall and then make an announcement. In that moment the last piece of treasured meat on the plate of a particular sibling would be snatched when everyone jumped up from their seats, screaming and looking up to see the scorpion. Such action was considered the ultimate choice for the victim who had caused the other siblings to be punished because of a past careless behavior.

Likewise adults are spiteful but can be more devious. They act in a passive aggressive manner. They will smile with you and work with you on a task, congratulate you too but as soon as your back is turned they will undo tiny parts of it or possibly destroy it after taking your know-how methods to be their own. The truth of the matter is they sometimes abhor to digest the fact that someone who is mediocre in their eyes can be smart.

Passive aggressive individuals remain in a constant yes mode but if you check their facial expressions you will find the real them. Don't adjust your lenses when it comes to passive aggressive individuals. Hold your focus when they tell you not to worry about a project you were helping them with because you have done enough. It's a sign that they are displeased with you about something pertaining to that project. Their aim at that time is to penalize you. Just like a spiteful person, passive aggressive feign innocence when they want you out of their sight for good. They keep you emotionally uneasy and to be a constant worrier. The minute you recognize a passive aggressive person or a cunning adult, do not make an alarm. Remain quiet to the point where you can hear a rat pissing on cotton; and be sure to keep a secret diary to protect you.

Saying: Han in a lion mouth, tek time draw it out.
Translation: Hand in lion's mouth, take time and pull it out.
Meaning: Whenever someone in power is looking for trouble, be discreet in your moves.

Is matrimony high stakes?

I recall a wise man from my childhood days who always suggested that people should "check breed" before entering into matrimony. His rationale behind his statement was: a person could be from a family of murderers, robbers, liars, beggars, lazybones, illnesses and little education. He had no time to entertain the saying, *love is blind* when it came to such observations. As far he was concerned the parties getting joined in holy matrimony should meet the following specifications: God fearing, sound mind, physically healthy, be from a respectable family, financially apt, believe in procreation and should not indulge in sexual intercourse before marriage.

In today's world some of his beliefs would be mocked and seen as ridiculous especially when it comes to not having sex before marriage. The talk is no one should buy *puss in a bag*. It's imperative to know that the sex is good before marriage. It's unimaginable to think that some people planning to get married would treat sex as if they are sampling foods or they are at a wine tasting event. Marriage is a commitment and should be taken seriously. Sexual intercourse isn't the only item that comes with marriage. A host of other things exist to make a good marriage. Respect, understanding and love are some of the other things. Love is key! And by the way in my opinion don't mistake a sexual encounter for love. Without love there will be a breakdown in the marriage which will lead to *it's over lane.* Done! Divorce! Bye boy! Bye girl! Go back to your mama and papa. And if they are not around, go back from whence you came.

Saying: Marriage a nuh food truck.
Translation: Marriage is not a food truck.
Meaning: Do not rush into marriage; wait until the time is right.

Are married women more spiteful than married men?

Foremost, married people should be the last to include the word spite in their lives. I am not a marriage counselor but I know well enough that as a couple they should set aside all disputes and work together. Using random names, here are two examples that could cause spitefulness in a marriage. 1) John arrived home at 11:00pm on Susan's, his wife, birthday. He explained that he was out with the boys and had no clue time had slipped by. Accepting the fact that he had made the biggest blunder in his life, he apologizes to Susan. Susan feeling deeply hurt refuses to accept his apology and needles him about his *forgetfulness* everyday thereafter. Our elders would have said she was like a setting hen, miserable. Have you ever seen a setting hen attacking people who get in its way? It's not a pretty sight as they defend themselves from a hard peck by kicking and screaming at the attacker. 2) Susan spends most of her time at church on Sundays and then goes back to night meetings three times a week. Susan who is firmly wrapped up in her faith believes that she has a right to go to her house of worship anytime, and stay for as long as it pleases her. Monday to Friday and twice on Sundays without interference from anyone, including her husband, John.

Keeping in mind that I am not a marriage counselor, would you agree that the two examples given are capable of wrecking any marriage? While the answer is being pondered, the interesting thing is that John thinks he did the right thing by apologizing to his wife, Susan, for arriving home tardy on her birthday. Susan also thinks that she is correct in defending her faith. It's interesting to see them defend their own rightness but still nothing is solved. Resentment remains a weapon between them. Eventually what will happen in their marriage is: Susan will not engage in any *bedwork* otherwise known as sexual activity and even refuse to prepare meals for her husband. The husband on the other hand will show the wife that she has the blade and he has the handle. So he goes ahead and discontinue his financial obligation to the household. And before you know it they both will be heading to splitsville without any hope of reconciliation. Would you, at this juncture, agree that It's best to give and take in relationships so that peace can reign? According to my mother, a woman should not spite a man by withholding sex and food from him because he will go elsewhere to be served.

In the same breath my mother advised me that every woman should have a secret savings account for use during *rainy days*. According to her not every truth should be known. Some husbands are spendthrift and cannot handle money properly. The savings could be kept anywhere: in a thread bag tucked away in the brassiere a woman is wearing, under the mattress or burried in a hole in the backyard. She also emphasized that a woman should take along *vex-money* when going out with her husband or significant other. *Vex-money* is also known as taxi fare. It's possible the female will need it to return home should an argument develop between her and her date.

Overall, respect is the key in any marriage. A woman should be respectful to her husband and matrimonial home, know when it's time to be at home. A man should be respectful to his wife and matrimonial home, not just his happy hour/bar friends, poker and domino partners. People who value relationships will try to avoid *spiteful lane*. It can be disastrous exploring it.

Saying: Yuh pair yuh nose fi spite yuh face.
Translation: You pair your nose to spite your
face.
Meaning: Acting out of resentment could bring
harm to yourself.

Do you practice good hygiene?

The people of old mantra was: *cleanliness is next to Godliness*. They covered their heads while cooking. They wore aprons or pinafores. They washed their hands often. They also washed their hands after using the latrine. They covered their mouths when they yawn. They covered their mouths when they coughed. They covered their sneezes. They carried handkerchiefs to clean hands and mouths, and as a receiver for contents released from nose. Fingernails were clipped short. Spoons were used to knead flour when making dumplings. They didn't speak over the foods they were preparing because spit balls do not discriminate. For the same reason, they did not hold conversations at the dining table while eating.

In every spheres of proper hygiene, those old timers were a force to be reckoned with. They kept their houses spic and span and instructed children to keep their bodies in the same manner. Get up in all the crevices and corners, behind the ears, up the nostrils and under the fingernails and toenails to get rid of grime. The nape of the neck should be scoured clean when taking a bath or shower because sweat and grease always lodge there in abundance. To see a ring formed out of perspiration and grease around the collar of a shirt, blouse or dress was definitely not a pretty sight to behold. The wearer would be coached on how to handle and protect their clothes. Inasmuch as washing the nape of the neck was important, some people showed cleverness by wearing a handkerchief over the collar of their garment; to protect it from residues that could prove difficult when doing the laundry.

Old time people had an astronomical hygiene checklist and even warned children and young adults to be careful about who they lie with or mix and mingle with. They were immensely against trying on or wearing other people's shoes and clothes. The fear of being afflicted with chigger, ringworm and lice was enough to scare children away from people's personal items. There was a rumor about an inquisitive woman who visited someone's house and had the audacity to powder her face from a container that was placed on the bureau. The powder was later identified as the ash of a relative.

In everyday living it is expected that we do our best when it comes to being tidy, clean and healthy. Some people will clean their houses with zest, interest, tender loving care for durability and for their wellness. Whereas some don't care about its condition. It wouldn't matter to them if cobwebs are plentiful and strong enough to strangle them. Neither do they care if they are buried in dust and grime. Neither do they care if any contagious illnesses are derived from their lackadaisical and selfish attitude. Granny would have said, *Misery loves company.*

Saying: An ounce of prevention is better than a pound of cure.

Meaning: Apply good measures whenever it becomes necessary. Don't let things get out of control.

Do you practice safe sex?

Modern times has seen its share of sexually transmitted diseases. The description, explanation and visual of the diseases are scarier than being in a haunted house. The revelation is enough to send us cowering and shielding our crotches and mouths or any orifice linked to the body from the awful attacks. Unfortunately, there are some people who believe that sex was invented in Hollywood and they are at will to indulge without thinking that something could go wrong. Sexual intercourse is not a game. It is to be taken seriously.

When it comes to practicing safe sex, there are myriads of information provided to guide and protect us. There are the prophylactic measures. Condoms are jazzy. They come with edible intentions to defeat the purpose so don't be fooled. There are various colors, some almost psychedelic from the disco era to spark interest among some men and women who oppose their use. They would do anything to prevent them from coming between them and their body. It is their belief that when having sex skin to skin feels best. In today's world who can you trust? Why take risks? Not everything can be seen with the naked eyes. Not all that glitters is gold. Some people engaging in sexual intercourse have become set in their microwave routine, giving credence that a condom isn't necessary. Grab! Bang! Done! By then in that short space of time, the horse had made its way through the gate and probably wreaked havoc.

You would be surprised to learn that some married people are of the opinion that there is no need to practice safe sex. And it is rightfully so because the marriage vows have expressed that the union is subjected to obedience and respect. In my opinion, the union is expected to consist of two people, not a union which allows for more than two to be gathered in one bed in the name of variety, spice, good time and an open-mind.

When it comes to an open-mind, the arrogance in some men makes it easy for them to mock safe sex. The story was told about a male who was pressured by his female partner to use a condom during sex. At the end of their coitus adventure in the woods, the male tossed the used condom. It landed on a barbwire fence in close proximity to them and where it remained swinging, pushed by the wind. The male looked at it, turned to his female partner and invited her to watch. After a few seconds he smiled and mentioned to her that the condom had great balancing skills because it had not fallen to the ground. He then pointed at the jacked-up condom and it contents, and in a bragging toned he mentioned, *That boy would have been a damn good acrobat. Look at him still swinging.* Clearly he was an arrogant man to have even determined the sex of his waste. His only interest was sexual stimulation and the measure of his ejaculation.

Saying: Yuh lie wid dawg; yuh rise wid fleas.
Translation: You lie with dog; you rise with fleas.
Meaning: Chose your company with car.

Is your wisecrack an insult?

Some people are so darn witty and full of sarcasm that they can tell you to go to hell in a straw basket or coconut shell and you would gladly do it, blazing all the way. I recall walking into an establishment with Sheila (not her real name), an acquaintance. As we walked towards the accessories rack, Sheila saw one of her friends.

"Good morning, Jill (not her real name)! She said with excitement.

"It's obvious", Jill responded, smiling and playing with her long fake black hair.

Sheila winced. Insulted by the response which has become popular, she looked at Jill and said, "You are such a bitch. Who are you trying to impress? You full a shit! You always insult people and try to pass it off as a joke".

Jill opened her eyes wide at Sheila as if she had seen a ghost.

"Why are you looking at me like that?" Sheila asked Jill. "You have a dirty habit and I hope you will put an end to it today. Because the next time you see me and try to show off before other people, I promise I'll thump you on your mouth to swell it up".

Jill looking on with shock opened her mouth to speak but the words must have lodged in her throat. Not a sound came from it as Sheila and I left the establishment in silence and to my relief.

Saying: Bullfrog seh wat is joke tuh yuh a death tuh mi.
Translation: Bullfrog said whatever is joke to you is death to me.
Meaning: The situations some people find as humor is critical to others.

Are you covetous?

It's not healthy to crave for possessions belonging to others. People with that attitude are labeled *red-eye* by the long ago people. Some people are so covetous that they will inveigle people's partners who are progressive to be with them. There are moral principles that govern a person's behavior. The teachings should be done at home from a tender age and backed up by worthwhile organizations.

Covetous behavior can lead to the destruction of the mind. It's a corridor to criminal activities and greed.

Saying: Yuh nuh noh how parson get him gown.
Translate: You don't know how a person acquired his gown.
Meaning: Don't covet people's belongings. You have no clue how they acquired them.

Do you feel free?

It's important to be free in mind, spirit and body yet it seems difficult to achieve because of all the public distractions going on around us and even those in our homes and lives. There are a myriad of things that people try to give them comfort: Some will escape to an island of sun, beach and sand to relax. But find that when they come back they will again face the situations that they tried to avoid. Some people will exercise. Some people will go shopping. Some people will cook and eat until they are uncomfortably stuffed. Or, according to the elders, *dig their graves with their own teeth*. Some people will pray. Some people will engage in sexual intercourse to release tension. Some people will seek the opinion of others on how to be free.

In my humble opinion if we should seek advice on how to feel free from worries, we first have to begin with ourselves. Search and ask ourselves if we are conditioned to receive opinions without being resentful or biased.

Saying: If yuh fraid a yeye; yuh will nevah nyam head.
Translation: If you are afraid of eye; you will never eat head.
Meaning: If you dwell on the good opinion of others you will never flourish.

What did your mother instilled in you during childhood?

Besides cultivating self respect, going to school topped my mother's list of the things she instilled in me. She reminded me as often as she could how important learning is. Reading a book was imperative but surprisingly it also served as punishment for poor behavior or if I became idle. Did your mother do that too?

My mother had also instilled in me that kissing boys would get me pregnant. She even went a little further to say I should stay away from boys because they suffer from swelling skin. I held those beliefs for a very long time. It turned out that kissing was the overture to having sexual intercourse and swelling skin meant an erection. She even instilled in me that, *a girl cannot do what the boys do and still be a lady.*

Summary: Parents will inject fear in their children to keep them on the right path.

What did your father instilled in you during childhood?

My father had instilled in me that a good education and good manners would take me anywhere in the world. He also instilled in me not to be wasteful. His favorite saying to me on that topic was: *Willful waste; woeful want.* And for the times that I didn't pay heed to such a saying, he would top it with: *You shall suck salt through wooden spoon if you continue with your nonsense.* That meant I would encounter hard times which would lead me to do the impossible.

Most frightening, though, my father must have been a psychic. I recall during the early sixties when laziness prevailed among my siblings and I, he would tell us that he wouldn't be surprised if someone invented a self-flush toilet to accommodate our lazy ways. To date I have not researched if during the early sixties self-flush toilets were invented anywhere in the world. My father was an avid reader and was always abreast with current affairs, events and party politics. So it's possible that he came across something pertaining to that. However, at this moment in time, I will just enjoy the belief that my father was futuristic. And that whatever he had instilled in me have been superb help and reference.

Summary: Parents will inject fear in their children to keep them on the right path.

Do you embrace science, discipline of ancestors or spirituality over religion?

My lips are sealed. Be it about science blah blah blah. Be it about discipline of ancestors blah blah blah. Be it about spirituality blah blah blah. Be it about religion blah blah blah. You are right blah blah blah. I am wrong blah blah blah. You are wrong blah blah blah. I am right blah blah blah.
Clash! My lips are sealed.

Summary: See no evil, hear no evil, speak no evil, do no evil.

If you were asked to list five whores what or who would they be?

While you think about your answers let me give mine. In this era of modern times, the harsh behavior from some leaders has distorted and misconstrued certain words, turning them into whores. If I were to give the names of such whores, they would be: money, power, sex, race, religion and party politics.

Saying: Di higher di monkey climb di more him bahine expose.
Translation: The higher the monkey climbs the more it exposes.
Meaning: People true colors are revealed when they are in high positions.

When was the last time you revisited nursery rhymes and memory gems?

Back in the day nursery rhymes and memory gems played an important role in a child's development. They instilled ethics and were fun to recite. As the years went by, I kept revisiting them.

Nursery Rhymes

With the exception of *Humpty Dumpty*, the egg, that sat its fragile bahine on a high wall to its detriment; my adult eyes found an undertone of sex, pervert and peeping tom among a few. Luckily the values, etiquette, and overall discipline gained from them throughout innocent years are so deeply cemented that not even a sledge hammer or backhoe can destroy them.

For example, through my adult eyes, the lively and beloved nursery rhyme *Wee Willie Winkie* has gone from a wanton child and street urchin to a pervert. He ran from house to house at nights, peeping through windows and keyholes at the ladies getting ready for bed and with the hope that he would get into their homes to seduce them. He was a village ram and must have been exhausted by daylight. The nursery rhyme *Jack Sprat* now leads me to throw it in the halls of oral sex. As a child I merrily thought Jack Sprat and his wife had been served a delicious meal which encouraged them to lick the platter clean, in the same manner that I used to lick leftover cake batter from the mixing bowl at home.

I am glad to have milked the nursery rhymes of all the innocent and redeeming qualities before adulthood.

Memory Gems

The memory gem *Bits of Paper* was a joy to sing. The teachers used psychology to instill cleanliness and organization:

> *Bits of paper, bits of paper*
> *Lying on the floor*
> *Make the place untidy*
> *Make the place untidy*
> *Pick them up*
> *Pick them up*

The memory gem associated with speaking the truth still lives on:

> *Speak the truth and speak it ever*

Cause it what it will
He who hides the wrong he did
Does the wrong thing still

The memory gem about education still lives on:

Labour for learning before you grow old
For learning is better than silver and gold
Silver and gold will vanish away
But a good education will never decay

The memory gem about effort and ambition still reigns:

Good better best
Never let it rest
Till your good be better
And your better best

Favorite sayings for the chaotic times

Saying: Yuh si a man's face but not im heart.
Translation: You see a man's face but not his heart.
Meaning: Sometimes the mouth doesn't always deliver what's in the mind.

+++++

Saying: Uneasy lies the head that wears a crown.
Meaning: People who govern or those who are with big titles have enormous responsibilities that can impede sleep and freedom.

+++++

Saying: Fingah nevah seh luk ya; it seh luk de.
Translation: Finger never says look here; it says look there.
Meaning: People do not see their own faults. They would rather point out the faults in others.

+++++

Saying: If fish comes from river bottom and broadcast that shark is down there, believe it. Meaning: Listen to the person who shares an experience.

+++++

Random words that could possibly shape questions:

A

ACQUAINTANCE
ANGER
APPEARANCE
ASSISTANCE
AUTOMOBILE

B

BANK
BANK CARD
BED
BEHAVIOR
BENCH
BOOK
BOSS
BROTHER
BULLY
BUS

C

CAREER
CARING
CHAIR
CHARACTER

CHEESE
CHOCOLATE
COFFEE
COLLEGE
COMPUTER
COMMONSENSE
CONCERNS
COUCH
COUSIN
CREDIT CARD
CRITIQUE
CRY
CULTURE

D

DEBT
DEPORTMENT
DIET
DISCIPLINE
DOCTOR

E

EMPLOYMENT
ENVIRONMENT
ETHIC
ETIQUETTE
EXERCISE

F

FACEBOOK
FAMILY
FINANCE
FRIEND
FURNITURE

G

GAMES OF CHANCES
GENDER
GOAL
GOD
GOSSIP
GUIDELINE

H

HAIR
HATE
HEALTH
HELP
HOARD
HOBBY
HONEST
HOSPITAL
HOUSE
HUMOR
HUSBAND

I

INSECURE
INTERNET

J

JOURNEY
JUSTICE
JUNK

K

KNOWLEDGE
KIND

L

LANDLORD
LAUGH
LAUNDRY
LIAR
LOVE
LIVING CONDITION

M

MANAGER
MANICURE

MANNERS
MASSAGE
MEDIA
MELANCHOLY
METICULOUS
MOOD
MONEY
MUSIC

N

NURSE
NUTRITION

O

ONLINE SHOPPING
ORGANIZED
OWN

P

PARTY POLITICS
PEDICURE
PHONE
POLITICIAN
PROFESSION

Q

QUIET
QUANT
QUARREL

R

RADIO
RECREATION
RELATIONSHIP
RELATIVE
RELIGION
RESPECT
RESTAURANT

S

SAD
SCHOOL
SELF
SELF ESTEEM
SEXUAL INTERCOURSE
SHARING
SISTER
SMILE
SOCIAL STATUS
STOCK MARKET
STORES
SUBWAY

T

TABLE
TAXI
TELEVISION
TEMPERAMENT
TRAIN
TRAIT
TWITTER

U

UBER
UMBRELLA
UNDERSTAND
UNIVERSE
UNIVERSITY

V

VACATION
VALUES
VICTIM
VICTORY
VOTE

W

WALK
WAR
WASTE
WIFE
WIG

WILL
WISDOM
WORK

X

XENOPHOBIA
XEROX

Y

YARD

YEAR

YIELD
YOGA

Z

ZEAL
ZODIAC
ZONE
ZOO

Noteworthy

Diplomacy is the art of saying nice doggie until you can find a rock. - Will Rogers. This quote was shared by a relative during a conversation.

Pretty Face and Bad Character. - Chaka Demus. This Jamaican Reggae song has been delivered via: airwaves, street vendors, events, parties and home stereo systems.

Money Money Money. - The O'Jays. This American song was delivered via: airwaves, street vendors, events, parties and home stereo systems.

Sayings/Proverbs/Adages: Shared by the elders, my parents and random people.....major grooming tool during childhood, major helper in adulthood.

Nursery Rhymes: Childhood obligation...a part of school curriculum.

Memory Gems: Childhood obligation...included in school curriculum.

Bible information: Childhood obligation...at school and church.

Sugarcane stall - Flatbush, Brooklyn, NY

Snow day - Flatbush, Brooklyn, NY

INDEX

Who can you trust to listen to your concerns? (Pg 38)

Do you take your troubles to God? (Pg 40)

Are you a silent speaker? (Pg 42)

Are you cautious? (Pg 46)

How are your coping skills fairing as the world turns and heaves its underwear? (Pg 47)

Are you about to go out of your mind because of people's behavior? (Pg 49)

Are incentives great encouragers? (Pg 50)

Can smart people do the wrong thing? (Pg 53)

Are you giving yourself good grades? (Pg 55)

What is your radar detecting? (Pg 57)

Should I focus on taking care of others before myself? (Pg 58)

Are you destructive? (Pg 60)

Are you a procrastinator? (Pg 62)

Are you putting yourself in harms way? (Pg 64)

Is peer pressure toxic? (Pg 66)

Is a tattletale readily accepted at home? (Pg 68)

Should a tattletale be given honor in the workplace? (Pg

69)

Should a team member be allowed to do the work of a manager? (Pg 73)

Have you been overlooked for a job that you had an interest in? (Pg 75)

Are you taking on more work than you can manage? (Pg 77)

When last have you had a conversation with yourself? (Pg 79)

Are you a giver? (Pg 82)

Is it difficult to decline someone's offer? (Pg 84)

Are you a taker? (Pg 85)

Is there comfort in being a liar? (Pg 87)

Do you have nimble hands? (Pg 89)

Do you believe in generational curse? (Pg 91)

How often are derogatory labels placed on a female? (Pg 93)

How often are derogatory labels placed on a male? (Pg 95)

Are you spiteful? (Pg 97)

Is matrimony high stakes? (Pg 100)

Are married women more spiteful than married men? (Pg 101)

Do you practice good hygiene? (Pg 105)

Do you practice safe sex? (Pg 108)

Is your wisecrack an insult? (Pg 111)

Are you covetous? (Pg 112)

Do you feel free? (Pg 113)

What did your mother instilled in you during childhood? (Pg 114)

What did your father instilled in you during childhood? (Pg 115)

Do you embrace science, discipline of ancestors or spirituality over religion? (Pg 117)

If you were asked to list five whores what or who would they be? (Pg 117)

When was the last time you revisited nursery rhymes and memory gems? (Pg 118)

Favorite sayings for the chaotic times (Pg 122)

Random words that could possibly shape questions (Pg 124)

Author

Name: Grace Asphall Nee Dunkley
Country of birth: Jamaica West Indies
Country of residence: United States of America
Marital Status: Widow (Husband served in United States army)
Occupation: Retiree
Previous Book: Memories Have No Editing Ability...a collection of poems
Blog: www.fromheretotherewithgrace.com
Interests: Interacting with all kinds of people. Absorb nature and its characters, especially rocks. Facebook. Humor. Books. Jewelry making. Dancing. Music. Travel.
Dislike: Confrontation
Immediate Family: 2 daughters, 6 grandchildren, 1 great grandchild.
Other Information: Cancer survivor since 2005.
Favorite public transportation: Train